The Gardener's Gold Ring

by Nancy Bopp

Illustrated by Christina L. Mutch

JOURNEY
FORTH™

Greenville, South Carolina

The Gardener's Gold Ring

Designed by TJ Getz

Greenville, SC 29614

Printed in the United States of America

ISBN 1-57924-722-9

15   14   13   12   11   10   9   8   7   6   5   4   3   2   1

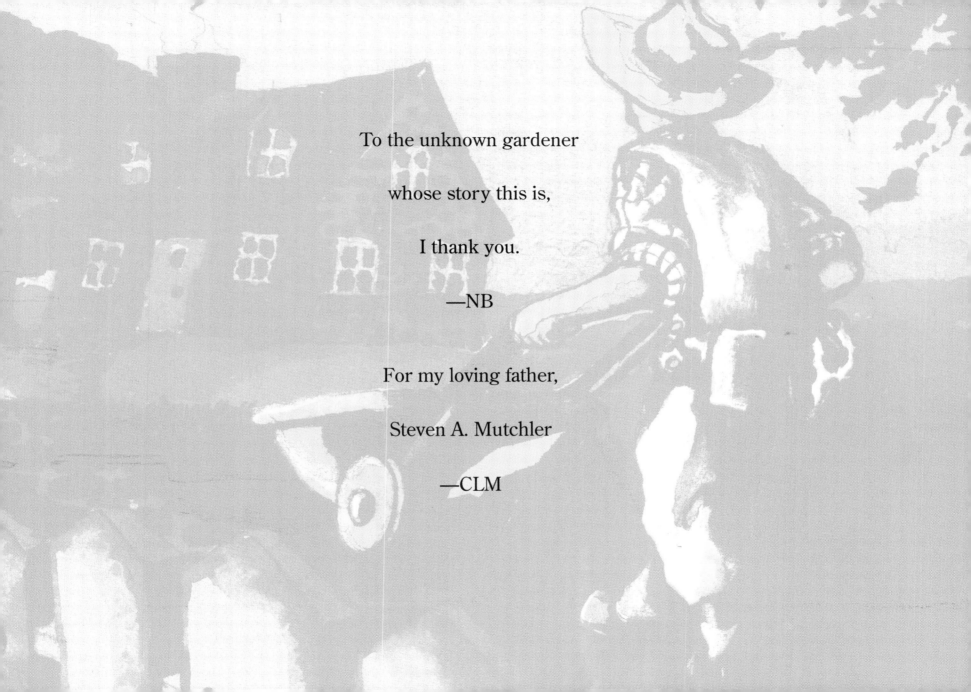

To the unknown gardener

whose story this is,

I thank you.

—NB

For my loving father,

Steven A. Mutchler

—CLM

Once not so long ago, a gardener lost his gold ring in the dirt.

He went to his wife. "Wife, this is hard to say. My ring is lost in the garden."

"Oh, Husband. Your wedding ring." The wife took his hand, and tears came to her eyes. "I cannot get you another."

All that evening the two hoed and raked to find the ring. By nightfall they were tired and had found nothing.

"Let us go to bed," said the gardener, "and tomorrow I will look again."

The next day he looked on his hands and knees. He dug through the dirt, uprooting a patch of flowers, but again found nothing.

The gardener was sad. His ring was gone. He thought of his wedding day, when his wife had slipped the golden circle on his finger.

"I cannot replace the ring," he said to himself, "but I can show her just how much I love her."

"I will plant for her a special garden. One to fill her cooking pots—a kitchen garden all her own!"

He set to work gathering seeds—seeds to grow carrots and corn, beans and basil, turnips and peas and tomatoes and squash—and planted them together around his beautiful flowers. The days were hot, but he watered and watched as the kitchen garden blossomed to green.

After a time the plants bore fruit. "Husband, you are a loving man," said the wife. "My garden is beautiful and useful too. Tonight we will eat from it."

That night she served roast beef with green beans and yellow squash for their supper.

They ate happily in the stillness of their home, to the music of their clock's tick-tock.

Days followed days, and meals followed meals until summer was done and fall harvest had come.

"I must bake a carrot cake," said the wife. "You should rest yourself, Husband, and when you awake we can celebrate our blessings."

The gardener went to sleep, and the wife went out to harvest carrots.

She grasped green and pulled up orange covered in dirt—one orange root. Up came another—two, and another—three, until the wife was humming at her task.

When the sixth carrot came up from the ground, the wife was startled and sat back on her heels. "What is this?" she said.

She gathered her carrots and hurried inside to hide what she had found. She cleaned the carrots and made a delicious cake.

"Husband, wake up! Our cake is ready."

The gardener got up and washed his face. "The first cake of autumn," he said smiling and sat down to enjoy himself.

"Wait," said the wife.
"I love you, and I
thank you for giving
me this garden," she
said. "Now the garden
thanks you too."

She turned and took a large orange carrot from its hiding place. She presented it to her husband, and right on the carrot was the gardener's gold ring!

"My ring!" said the gardener.
"What a wonder!"

Said the wife, "What a carrot!"

And together they laughed and
ate their cake with thankful hearts.